Danny the Farting Bunny. A Funny Read Aloud Story About Hidden Talents.

Rhymes: Carly-Anne Phillips, Hugh L. Macy
Illustrations: Soumya Choubey

ISBN: 9798414768036

Do you want to hear something really funny?
A tale about special but a bit stinky bunny?

He had a bottom, like you and I,
but smelt so rotten, it would make you cry!

How could something so stinky
come from something so small?
His bottom
has always been
so unpredictable!

He made sounds that squeaked,
and sounds that popped,

with a stench so bad
that would make your ears flop!

Poor little Danny...
with a behind he couldn't tame,
his brothers always made him feel so ashamed!

You see, his brothers had talents,
that were just so cool,
they were always
showing off after school.

He had a brother who's sense of smell
was something out of this world!
Even in the thickest of snow,
he could use his nose
to sniff out the loveliest carrot in the meadow.

and a brother
who's eyesight
was so precise,
he could spot a predator
and save your life.

DANGER-
DANGER!

Now, his last brother
was popular,
but to say he had a talent
was going too far.
See, he was good looking
and knew it too!
The bunny girls
crowded around him
like flies on poo.

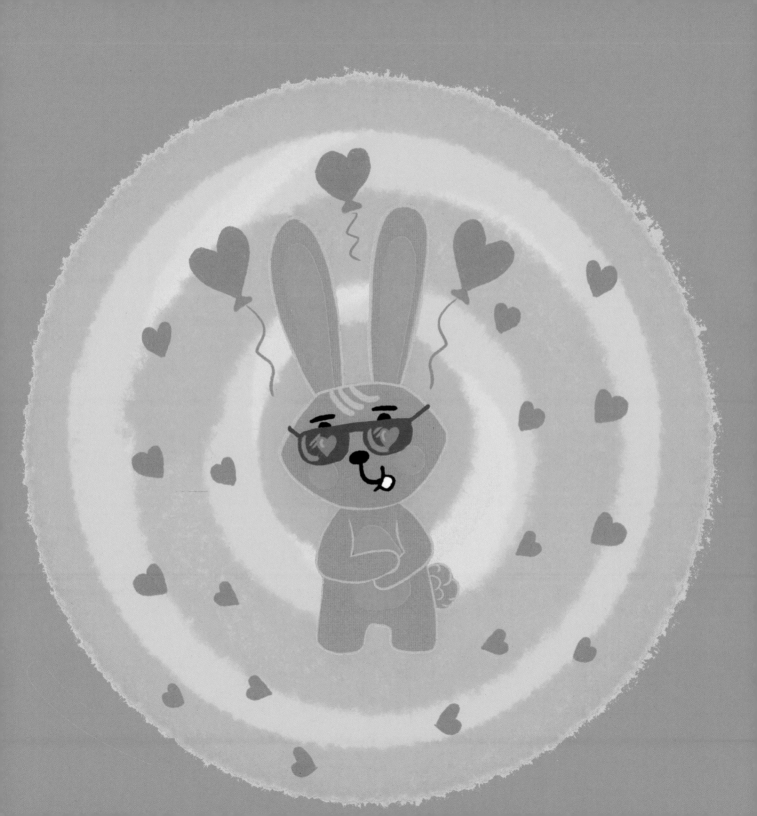

To Danny, passing winds
was no joke
but his brothers pointed,
they laughed and they
poked.

So poor little Danny,
his gassy ways
were leaving him
in a hoot,

all the time
he struggled
to hold in the toot.

But he had had enough!
He didn't care if it felt rough,
it was time to hold it in,
for real this time,
because every time he pffffft
it felt like a crime.

NO MORE FART!

So that's it! He held tight,
with all his might!

Nothing was going to slip by!
Alright!

As the day went,
Danny's belly ached,
But he had to persevere,
he would not break.

It was after school,
Danny and his bros,
were hopping their way home.
As usual Danny barely spoke,
as they were taunting
and taking turns to provoke,

Amid the teasing and the noise,
the boys were distracted,
they had no idea
a trap had been constructed.
Ahead of them all something so cruel...
A fox was waiting
for them to fall.

And fall they did
into a ditch.
The fox laughed a wicked laugh,
his sly eyes twitched!
With fear. the bunnies shudder,
as the fox got closer and closer,
Danny's stomach began to rumble
like thunder.

The fear of the fox
scared the bunnies to the core,
and Danny couldn't hold it in anymore!

What happened next
you could call it heroic,
Danny's gas bundle erupted
like something volcanic.
Like a pressure cooker,
his tummy shook shook!
Danny knew
what he must do,
so he held onto his brothers
tightly
and waited for the fox
to get nearer…
..ever so slightly.

Then he let it rip like a volatile bomb!
The fox was hit with a diabolical pong
and they blasted up into the air,
leaving the fox in a ditch of gastric despair.

BOOM!

FUSSS!

BAN

What a relief,
they fly through the sky!
The brothers can't believe
their eyes!
How could this happen?
How could this be?
As they ponder
and land safely.

Our brother is a hero!
Hip hip hooray!
And that's the story of when
Danny saved the day.

Now Danny is proud,
he holds his head high,
bunnies whisper as he hops on by.
''Danny's talent is remarkable,
he defeated a fox
that was this tall!''

They say he can sing a song,
for a minute long,
but not from his mouth,
but from somewhere down
south...

A farting talent may seem absurd
but forget what you have heard
because you have to understand
that little Dan
discovered bravery in his heart
that he can be
the bunny he was meant to be.
Do you agree?

So many talents are in
the world!
And which is yours?
I cannot tell.
But dare to be special,
don't be afraid
being yourself, like Danny,
the Brave.

Talents come in all shapes and sizes.
Some are quiet and some win prizes.
You could be magnificent at dancing
or fantastic at art
…while some can let off the most
extraordinary…fart!

POP POP!

BOOM BOOM!

Thank you for reading!

We have a great gift for you:

A FAMILY BOOK OF ABSOLUTELY USELESS ADVICES

To get your free copy , go to:

www.serenitypublish.com

Made in the USA
Columbia, SC
11 April 2022

58845251R00020